Salvation
From
A
Cell

By: Taveras Coleman

Salvation From A Cell
By: Taveras Coleman AKA DJ Mr. Famouz
Copyright: March 2024

Table of Contents

Chapter One
"Living In the Projects"

I grew up in the Marydale Housing Projects. Like any other kid growing up in the projects, surely you can imagine life was very hard for me as a child. When I say hard, I mean rough, because every day you were going to get tested. Whether it was at school or in the projects, you had to know how to fight. I had a bad attitude from the start, I was a little mean child; so, it didn't really matter to me, if somebody wanted to fight, I was ready! It wasn't because somebody was trying to test me that made me that way though, it was growing up in a household with a single mother and no father present. I won't say that was the sole reason, but I do believe, not having my real father in my life made me bitter. At a young age, I was developing a bad attitude. I believe it was based off what I saw growing up.

My mother had a boyfriend who was physically abusive. I was 5 years old at the time and there was constant fighting going on, and it troubled me a lot. It troubled me so much; to the point of having hate inside of me. I was full of anger and frustrated, because I was just a little kid, who wanted to protect my mom, but couldn't like I really wanted to. I remember, one night we came back from the store and when we got home, my mom was afraid that my stepfather could be hiding in the house. He was not supposed to be there, but he was, we didn't know that at first though. As me and my little brother walked through the apartment, we went into our bedroom, which was down the hall.

and turned on the light and looked around, we didn't see my mom's boyfriend. My mom suddenly asked, *"Did we see him?"* and I said, *"No Ma!"* Soon as I looked up, there was my mom's boyfriend at the top of the closet, coiled up like a snake. Suddenly, he jumped down off the top shelf and started running behind my mom. I was thinking to myself, what could I do to help. He ran outside behind my mom and started to fight with her in the middle of the street. So, I immediately ran back inside and grabbed a broom, then ran back outside and started hitting him in the back of the head. I was hoping with me hitting him in the head, it would stop him, but apparently it didn't. He took the broom out of my hand and started hitting my mom with the same broom. That just made me angry; so angry that I jumped on him hitting him with my hand. All of a sudden, somebody grabbed me from the back and pulled me away, then pulled him off my mom.

From that day on, something changed in me, and I was never the same after that. It just seemed like once that happened my anger grew worse. My mom would later tell me that, *"I had a very bad temper."* Little did she know, where it was coming from was because of him. I didn't know how to resolve those anger issues inside of me. So, from that point on I personally believe, that's where the mind of a killer was developed in me!

Chapter Two:
"The Day My Grandfather Died"

Unfortunately, even after my mom was abused by her boyfriend, she didn't leave him. He ended up moving back into the house again and we seemed like a normal family again. My mom bought me a BB gun for Christmas that year. Around that time, I started getting fascinated with guns, I didn't see a lot of guns at the time, but I knew they existed. I wanted a BB gun, so I got one. Little did I know getting a BB gun; I would end up loving to pull the trigger.

I remember one day in the projects; I had a friend by the name of Tyrone who was partially deaf, he used to wear one hearing aid in his ear. We were all playing the game of hide and go seek one day and I heard my brother, my sisters and some of my friends come running from around the apartments yelling and screaming, they were yelling, *"Tyrone is coming behind us."* At that moment, not knowing what happened, I ran in the house and got the BB gun. I had already been doing targeting practice, by shooting my little cousin in the hand. He would always dare me to shoot him in his hand, to see if I knew how to shoot accurately. So, I was ready to shoot Tyrone! As all of them were running past me, I stood in the middle of the yard and pointed the gun at Tyrone. I shot him in the stomach. I was just 6 years old. Immediately after, I dropped the gun and ran because Tyrone started screaming and hollering from the pain of that BB. I went and hid from my mom inside of our neighborhood convenient store, that my cousin named Cussie owned. Shortly after that, my mom came in there and found me. That was a painful day for me. My mom whipped the hell out of me. Then my stepfather cracked the BB gun over his knee in front of me and I cried like a baby. All I could hear her saying was, *"GET YOUR S**T!"* *You're going to live with your grandfather."* I packed all my clothes up, got in the back of the station wagon, and it pulled off. I was looking back like Tre from the movie**, "Boyz N The Hood!"**

My grandfather, who was a Pastor, also had guns; four of them to be exact, a garden, and he lived on a plantation by the University. I enjoyed going by his house, but now I was going to be staying over there, with him and my grandmother. My grandfather would take me to church with him. I would travel with him to every church he'd go to, on every Sunday morning. At times, during the night, he would take me and put me on his knee, while reading the bible to me. One Psalm in the bible that stood out the most to me, was Psalms 27. I didn't know what it meant. I really didn't know what the bible was about at the time, I was young. By this time, I was about 6 or 7 years old, somewhere around there. My grandfather and I would be around each other every day. My Paw-Paw had his bad habits; smoking cigarettes and whiskey drinking, but little did I know, he was sick. I did not know all the things that were going on with his health at the time.

One Sunday morning, me and my grandfather were coming out of a church, getting ready to go to another church he Pastored. As he was walking down the steps of the church and began to walk down the sidewalk to the car, suddenly he grabbed his chest and fell on the hood of one of the cars in the parking lot. When I looked back and saw my grandfather's face, I was terrified. I tried to run and save him, but the deacons of the church held me back. I stood there with tears in my eyes, watching them pull my grandfather away. That same day he went to the hospital, and I heard nothing about him for a couple of days. I thought he was coming home, but unfortunately, he didn't. A c ouple of days had passed by, and my mom picked me up from the bus stop one day after school. When I got into the car, it was very quiet. I asked her about Paw-Paw, She looked at me with tears in her eyes and said, *"Baby, He's gone!"* It broke my heart that day! I was already dealing with a lot of anger issues from being in the home with my mom and her abusive boyfriend. I'm angrier, more than ever now! I'm not just angry with people, I was angry with God!

Chapter Three
"Gangsta Nerd"

My life had to move on and the only person that I thought or looked up to as a father, was my grandfather and he's gone. Now, I really don't know who I am. Like, I was a kid, whose identity was lost, and all this was going on inside of me. One minute, I wanted to be a good boy, that did good things, like a good child supposed to be. Then there was the other part of me, that was a low-down rotten, sinister kid, that couldn't be trusted. They used to call me Bam-Bam. If anyone knows about the Flintstones cartoon; of course, now that tells you, how old I am. *(Laughs)*. Bam-Bam was the little bad boy who was always messing up stuff. That was me. JUST BAD! I was conflicted with the part of me that wanted to be good and the other part that wanted to be evil. I found myself trying to be somebody of the streets, even in the young ages of my life, and that should not have been going on inside of me; but it was.

I remember being teased for wearing glasses, I was a smart kid in school, but I was the class clown and wanted to start trouble too. I don't know whether, it was that I came from the projects, that made me feel like, I had to act up or not. But I did! It could have been just my own issues in my mind, that I couldn't solve at the time. I wanted to be a gangster. A gangster that was smart though. I didn't want to be a dumb gangster. I wanted to do things that were more organized. I didn't really get into the streets immediately, but I did dance around them for a while. I was very familiar with them, because as my mom moved in different places, we moved into areas that were very rough. Even though we were out of the projects, we found ourselves in different places and cities with rough neighborhoods. Some places that we moved in were good, and it didn't have a lot of criminal activities going on, but we would bring that bad environment to the area. I mean, we would be the only kids in the area doing all kinds of crazy stuff.

I remember around 11 years old, I got arrested for a burglary. Me and my friend, (he passed away now), along with my little brother, pretty much robbed the post office. We took all the money that was inside the gift cards during Christmas time. Then took all the cards and spread them all over the streets. That's how we got caught! We took the money out the cards and just threw the cards on the ground on Canal Boulevard. We didn't care; man, we were wild! The police eventually caught up with us, put us in the back of the car and brought us home. We were too young to be charged with a federal crime, but it was a federal crime we committed. They could not charge us federally. So, we ended up on state probation me and my little brother. My first brush with the law and I was only 11 years old, on probation. My homeboy, who passed away, he went to juvenile detention because, he was already on probation. That was the beginning of my trouble with the law and into the criminal justice system. Little did I know, my future would look like this from this day on.

Chapter Four
"Wild Child On The Loose"

I'm a teenager now. Nobody could tell me anything! Still going to school, but now I'm introduced to something that's going to really change my life around. My sister's boyfriend at the time was a barber, and I would go by the house, to get my haircut. I would see her boyfriend's friends there, who at the time was coming to get their hair cut too. They were coming in cars with rims, gold teeth in their mouth and with jewelry all over them. As a kid, I didn't have no job. I was a teenager, I had an attitude, but I still was broke! Seeing them pull up like that, I said, *"That's what I want to do."*

One day I went to get my haircut and I see something on the stove cooking. I didn't know what it was at the time, but I saw a glass inside of the pot. It was something inside that glass. I just so happened to look in there and said, *"What is that?"* Come to find out later, it was crack cocaine that was being cooked. I wanted in, but they were telling me, *"No, you need to stay in school!"* That's how I got the name, gangsta nerd. They would say, *"I was a gangster nerd because, I was smart in school, but I really wanted to get in them streets."* I already had a charge on me from the post office, but I'm seeing quick money now. These boys got rolls of money. I tried to get in. I tried to ask them. I would ask them to let me get in, "No!" they kept saying to me. So, I said, *"I'll find the way!"* and that's what I did! I went to the projects across town, we called THE OPJ, that's how I got in. I don't remember where I got it from, which is not important anyway, but that night I spent $60 dollars. At the time, we called it a double up or flipper because you could flip your money; spend $60, get $120. If you're a hustler, you could get $200 or more. It was a way you can use that razor blade and cut the rocks to make more from what I had, that's how I learned the drug game.

That same night, I was trying to make a sale and not knowing how the drug game really worked, some crack smokers pulled off with my crack. I'm not going to lie, that right there, flipped a switch in my mind. You must realize, I already knew how to pull the trigger from the BB gun, plus already having anger built up inside of me. Y'all gone play with me like this? So, that night I took that loss, but I got me a gun. I said to myself, *"I'm not about to play with nobody anymore!"* As I began to get deeper in the dope game, I started selling weed at school, plus selling crack every night. Staying out all night, doing what I wanted to do. Eventually, I got busted on a marijuana case at my neighbor's house. I would've got busted with the crack too, but I was able to flush it down the toilet before the narcotic agents came in. I was going to jump off the balcony, but I was like nope, "I'm not about to hurt myself, I'm not breaking my bones. I was only 15 years old, turning 16 that year.

The police took me to jail. My mom didn't even know what was going on because, I got arrested at somebody else's house upstairs *(Laughs).* I ended up in jail and this time, I got a new case. The same night, I got arrested again. Now, that was crazy! but it was not stopping me though. I was still doing crazy things. I ended up stealing my mom's car, me, and my little brother, just to go joyriding. I started to rent out rock rentals -if you don't know what "rock rentals" is, that's when somebody who smokes crack and rents out their car for "rocks," that's what we called it. I would have their car all day. We would tear the people cars up. Dogging them out. Selling dope in them and even racing in them, just doing all kinds of stuff in those people cars. I had found a new passion and that was selling dope. I thought to myself, *"This is going to be my life to forever!"*

Chapter Five
"Menace To Society"

I believe it was around the time when the movies **"Boyz in The Hood**" and **"Menace to Society,"** had come out, two movies that I used to love watching. I was young and wild in the mind, acting like a fool, not giving a dam about nothing or nobody! I was getting deeper into them streets, all while in high school trying to graduate. I was all the way over my head in the drug world now. I'm in school, but I was still hanging in the streets all night. When I say all night, I mean all night, all the way until sunrise and then to school after being up all night. So, at this time, I was getting my hands on more drugs and more criminal activity and my favorite "guns." I went from getting a possession of marijuana case, to being on probation. Then, right when I finished probation as a juvenile, I was turning 17; I was then charged with distribution of crack cocaine. Yes, selling crack and when I got busted! I STILL DID'NT SLOW DOWN!

I got arrested, it was my first felony case as an adult. Even though I was incarcerated at the time after I was busted, my mind never left the streets! I was in jail learning how to be smarter. at what I was doing. I remember writing my mother a letter telling her, *"I wish I could tell you I want to change, but I don't. I told her I'm going to be a "gangster for life."* So, while I'm in jail talking to the older convicts, learning how to do time; they were teaching me how to create shanks, that's (homemade knives) to defend myself and how to fight certain ways, while I was in jail. They didn't teach me how to fight a regular fight, they taught me guerilla warfare; how to kill a person or cut them up bad and I'm only 17 years old! I stayed in jail about a month and then I bonded out. Nothing had changed, I went right back out in them streets again!

This time, I went from selling dope to a life of robbery. I was putting on ski masks now. I'm taking it to another level. I'm watching movies, that's showing me how this robbery stuff goes and I'm going to do this right here in this city. Me and my Lil Partners, started robbing people. Dressing up in all black, and ski masks. We weren't just robbing people in my city, but we were robbing people in other cities as well. All night me and my boys would ride looking for people to rob, preferably other drug dealers. I could sit here and tell you a lot of stories, but it would only land me in jail, so I will plead the fifth. Just know that now, I didn't care. I'm all the way deep in them streets even hanging with older dudes, that rob and kill. I'm starting to lead a gang now. A gang, that I pretty much put together myself. We didn't have crips and bloods in the city at the time, but we started it. It started off from a friend of mine, I knew from Los Angeles, California. I started wearing a rag around my head, wrists and ankles representing this new so called gang life, I've created. I started leading my friends on how to rob, shoot or whatever it took for them to get things done and make it happen. It was for INITIATION!

Chapter Six
"Made Man"

Now since I was the gangster that I thought I was, I ended up going back to jail on that same drug case because I missed my court date. I stayed out all night, selling crack and drinking with my friends. We were young, like 17, 18, and 19. I forgot I had to go to court. I had a warrant out for my arrest for contempt of court, so when I found out, I turned myself in. When I went to court, the judge sentenced me to 7 years hard labor in prison! I said, *"Hold up, Sir "I'm in school, I can't do 7 years!"* Apparently, the judge saw my juvenile record and said*, "It was time for me to do some time!* I talked to the lawyer that day who was representing me while we were in court, to go and talk to the judge and help me with my case.

My lawyer at the time, went up to the judge's bench and talked to him and I ended up getting a year in jail, which was my senior year in high school. The seven years that were supposed to be given to me; the court suspended that. That's how the court system worked at that time. They suspended the time and gave me jail time for that year. So, 5 years' probation with a 7-year suspended sentence was what I received that day. If I broke the probation in 5 years, I would have to go back and do those seven years. In Louisiana at that time, if you violated your probation, you would do 3 and ½ years on 7 years with the possibility of getting paroled for good behavior. So, I was able to get one year in jail, that's about 6 months in jail because of how they sentenced you and then go back on probation when I came home.

I'm doing time now, so I must ride it out until I could go home. While I was in jail, I picked up a book. It was about John Gotti who was at the time, a Mafia boss out of New York. The book was so interesting because, I was already in a life of crime, but it was more on the organized level. Like I said before, that was me. I was the nerd. I always wanted to be the organizer, rather than do it all loose and wild, and not caring. I wanted something real and solid. I read that book and I was able to see how they were able to organize the crime families and what it meant to be a Made-man and what kind of initiation it would take to be that man. I told myself, this is how I'm going to live when I get home. So, when I got out of jail, I had a welding job making good money, at the time it was about $15 an hour. I was working from 3pm to 5am in the morning. I would leave the projects and go to work. My mama moved back into the same projects I was raised in. At this time, I was 18 going on 19 years old.

Shortly into the job, I got fired. So, I was back out in the streets quick. Instead of me waiting for another job or looking for another job, I said, I was going to do what I knew best. I'm about to get back robbing again. We started robbing people in the projects. I created a sawed-off shotgun and started robbing people - taking them out their cars. I used to wear a bullet proof vest. I was crazy! I realized that to be the Made-man I saw in the book about the initiation of the mafia, I had to step up my crimes. Not to brag or say what I did in that life of crime, but know this at this time, it's when I finally put the blood from another man on my hands, 'REDRUM."

Chapter Seven
"I'm On A New Level Now"

My life is totally different now because I have given my all into this criminal life. I was always sacrificing, plus now I have a man's blood on my hands. I've gained a reputation for somebody who likes to rob, shoot, and kill people. I had a crew; I use to hang with that was my little click from growing up. We ended up doing a robbery together one night and I didn't like how that went down. The robbery went bad that night and I got shot. After that I felt like, I couldn't trust them anymore. They were supposed to do their part and they left me stranded. So, I broke away from them. I ended up going solo for a while. It was hard trusting anyone with that kind of responsibility because it was so dangerous!

This was right about the time I'm starting to take trips to Houston, to come and see my family on my dad's side. My dad was living in Houston at the time. He was Colombian, but he was living in Houston. My sister's place was where I would go to when I got there. Houston, at that time was known to be the "DRUG CAPITAL," for us boys in Louisiana. I was getting on greyhound buses coming to Houston to find out where I could get marijuana, cocaine, and crack to bring back home to sell. I ended up making a connection with the Mexican Mafia. I was getting loads of drugs being sent back to where I'm from. I would even travel with them on my body, ducked taped down from my neck to my legs. Now you got to understand, I'm getting bigger packages of drugs, which is elevating me now. I'm soaring to a new level from being a person selling crack and robbing, to now being a drug kingpin. Making a name for myself in that life felt so good. But you do know what comes with rising in any area of your life, *"HATERS"* Yes, who want to take you down. So, eventually I started to get more police harassment with what I had going on because somebody was telling!

One night, I went to eat at a pizza place, to celebrate my daughter's birthday, suddenly I got a message that the police had kicked in my mom's door. I wasn't at home at that moment, but somebody had told the narcotic agents, I was keeping drugs somewhere in the backyard because that's exactly where they went looking. At this time, it was a song out by Puff Daddy, Mase & Notorious BIG called, *"More Money More Problems!"* I started seeing that having more money only brought on more problems. People I was close to, started doing evil stuff behind my back. I'll be honest with you, this is when I started to tell myself, I need to get out of this life. Even though I was rising in the game, I felt like I was falling in the same game. It was amazing to see, how I attracted so many haters. I couldn't believe how MANY OF THEM WERE CLOSE like REAL CLOSE! It was time for a change.

Chapter Eight
"It Was A Bad Night"

Nighttime was my thing, always dressed in black. I would sleep during the day and be in the house, but when night came that was my time. At this time, it was no turning back I'm doing any and everything from robbing, stealing carjacking, snorting coke, snorting heroin. I don't think there was anything I was not doing except putting a crack pipe in my mouth.

At nighttime, the clubs would be the hot spots for me. I used to like going out by the clubs because normally that's where the money was, but sometimes I didn't especially if it was a place, I didn't feel comfortable going in. One night, my boy Corey saw me sitting on the back of my car outside in the parking lot on St Charles Street, where I use to sell dope. He stopped and asked me to come out to a club, that was in another city. I really didn't want to go. My mind was more on making money, rather than going to a club that night. I really wasn't trying to go out anyway that night, because something felt strange in the air, like something bad was going to happen! On top of that, I didn't want to miss no sales from the dope fiends *(Laughs);* I felt like, if I was in the club, I would miss out on my money.

So, I didn't want to go. I don't know what made me end up going that night, but I ended up going anyway. Corey and some other people he came with, had already left. Even though I went; I still felt weird like something bad, was about happen. When I got there, there were so many cars. This club was known for shootings. People would get shot, some were even getting killed and so, I didn't like that spot. At that time of my life, I was known for being a murderer in the streets. That's why I knew good and well this was not the type of club, I needed to be at. As I pulled up and I was trying to find a parking spot, my homeboy and some of the people he was with was up in the club when I got there. I decided to stay outside and check out the girls that were walking in the parking lot.

All I can remember was a shootout started, so I started shooting because everybody else was shooting. I didn't know what was happening at first, because everybody was shooting. Everybody was running wild. The girls were screaming. As everything started to calm down, I could hear the sirens coming. I finally ended up getting the news that Corey was dead, he had got shot in the chest coming out of the door of the club! Man, that right there messed me up bad!

He was one of the first people I initiated in the gang with me, we did a lot of things together and that was my dawg. Now, he was dead! That week was his funeral, and I went to pay my last regards to the family. For some odd reason at the funeral that day, when the preacher was preaching, he kept looking at me hard, while he was delivering his sermon. I had been drinking liquor and smoking a lot weed that day, just to numb the pain I was feeling inside. I was going from gin to vodka, to weed back and forth, but I could not stop the pain, that I was feeling. I couldn't believe that someone this close to me had died. I mean a lot of friends had died, but not like this. We were together almost every single day growing up. We were like brothers. This broke my heart. I had started wondering, if something like that happened to him, what could happen to me. I'm already deep in this life with the criminal activities involving guns. It was just a matter of time!

At this time of my life, I'm all confused, I didn't know which way to turn, but to God! After going to the funeral and seeing the way things were happening around me. I asked God or rather I told him because I didn't know him at the time, so I just threw it out there and said, *"God I know that it must be more to life than this, because if this is what it's all about going back and forth to jail and dying. I don't want this life no more!"*

Chapter Nine
"I Knew There Was Something Missing"

Five years of probation and I'm trying to make it all the way to the end, but I'm messing up so bad. It just seems like, I couldn't stop. I was back out robbing again! I was back out in them streets with the murder mentality for real. I got a whole new crew who was about that murder life. Some real killers. We would be around each other every day. Snorting cocaine, snorting heroin, and drinking liquor, at this moment of my life, I'm severely mentally depressed and I'm just being ignorant, but I don't care about life anymore. My hope is gone. My friends are dying. I'm on these serious drugs and it's getting worse.

My attitude is getting worse. Me and my children's mother are constantly arguing every day, and on top of that, she was pregnant again! Now, I'm about to have my second child with her and I'm finding myself at times going to pray by the church that was next door to where we lived. I didn't think I could go to church at the time, because I felt so dirty, but not because of my clothes. It was my mind! I felt so evil. I thought God didn't want me around the church or the people in the church. I would say to myself, these people don't want me in the church. They knew me. They knew what I was about. How am I going to walk up in that church like this, is what I was saying to myself. So, I never went. I would just sit in front of the church and pray and wonder what was going to happen with my life. My friend was gone, and somebody had already put a hit out on me, over some rumor about a robbery, they assumed I committed. Apparently, the hit got called off because some kind of way, the hitman found out who I was connected to. I recognized later in my life; it was God who really protected me because He had a plan for my life. I can honestly say, that at this time of my life, I know I needed to come to God, but how?

This was my last year of probation and now I was facing a new drug case. Possession of cocaine! Another felony! I bonded out, while I was still on probation. Then a few months later, another felony case; it's possession of a firearm. These cases were piling up all in a few months of each other. It's my last year on probation, if I violate, I must do those 7 years, plus whatever I will get for these new charges! That didn't stop me though! At this point I think I'm John Gotti for real. I'm moving around, just as I read about him in the book. Committing crimes like never before. It was so much going at that time. So many stories, I could go on and on about, but some stories are not ever to be told.

I remember that night I got the firearm case. I had the police on a high-speed chase. I threw out the crack & cocaine, but the gun, they charged me with it. I threw the drugs, but somehow, they only found the gun. That still makes me shake my head to this day. Now, it's August; just a month later after I was arrested for the gun, I'm on the run from the police for two counts of 2nd degree murder. I ended up getting arrested in New Orleans, Louisiana and placed inside of Orleans Parish Prison. The arrest was for traffic violations, so, I tried to lie and give the officer my brother's name, hoping to get out quicker, but after the fingerprints came back, they said to me, *"You're not going anywhere!"* *We got you for murder!"* Now I'm locked up with all the rest of the murderers in New Orleans. I guess that's where I started realizing life was about to change for me; because I done reached the "BIG M," the murder charge. I'm sitting in that jail cell with about eight people, in a four-man cell. I'm on the floor with a blanket and its cold as a freezer. The food was horrible, it was an old bologna sandwich that was hard and cold. It didn't look good for me, and it didn't look like I was going home no time soon. This would be my final brick wall; I couldn't get through. My time in the streets had finally come to an end.

Chapter Ten
"My Visitation With God"

While I was currently being held on a murder charge at the Orleans Parish Prison, I was waiting to be extradited back to Thibodaux. It was where the crime was committed and the city where I was raised partially. As I was being transported back to the parish jail in Thibodaux, I started praying. I don't remember what them prayers were at the time, but all I know was that I was talking to God more than normal. I remember when the officers brought me into the jail, they did not put me in general population around the other inmates.

I was placed in a maximum-security cell alone; in which at that time, we called it the' 'Hole." There were no windows, nor light, except for the one that was inside the cell, that I had to pull the string to turn on. There was just a little area where I could slide the food tray in and out of. I used to be curious about this cell because I had been in jail a lot of times before this new case. I had known about this cell and even heard about it before, but never knew what it looked like inside. Finally, I was able to see the inside of that cell and how a person could live in here. Just never thought; I would have to see it this way. I knew because of the new murder case; I probably was never going home again.

So, I had to make it comfortable. It was very cold in there, it felt like a dungeon or a cave. I was by myself, so I was able to sleep without the constant all-night noise from the other inmates. When I got there, I was still high from mixing powder cocaine and heroin, with marijuana and smoking it. This had become my drug of choice which we called it, "speed balling in the streets." I was out of my mind, and tripping. It was somewhere during one of the days I was in there, I began pleading with God; that if He let me get out this time, I would start a music career and leave the streets alone. I already had offers from Cash Money Records, to come with them. This was at the time Lil Wayne was joining the label, but I never went. I was too deep off into the drug life and the other criminal activity, I was involved in. I was pretty much doing everything they were talking about in the rap music at the time. but now I'm trying to make this deal with God. If He let me out, I'll leave it all alone and just do music. As I was speaking that out of my mouth; suddenly right in the corner of my eye, in the corner of that room; a light appeared out of nowhere! It was a light that was so bright, that it looked like it had fire coming out of it.

As it got closer to me, I heard a voice say to me, *"No you're not, you're about to work for me."* At that moment, I just fell on my knees, and began to cry uncontrollably for a long time; it felt like I couldn't stop. And so, I said, *"Lord, I surrender my life to you, I give it all to you; I will serve you to the day that I die."* It wasn't about me making pleas with Him no more. It wasn't about me making deals with Him no more. It was me finally seeing that, I needed to give my life to God. That light, I had just saw suddenly disappeared. It was gone just like that. Little did I know, I just had a visitation from God. The next day, I was finally able to get a phone call to my mom and my children's mother. They had been threatening to call the local newspaper; to investigate why I could not use the phone, up until then, I had not been able to call anyone. So, I finally got that phone call and was able to talk to my mom. She told me that my aunt, my grandfather's sister, who was an

Evangelist, had been praying for me. She was a Missionary also a n d she traveled preaching and had a strong relationship with the Lord. She got on the phone with me, and she said, *"Taveras I've been praying for you."* and she said, *"The Lord told me to tell you, to give your life to Him."* And I told her, *"Auntie, I just did. I just gave my life to Him*!" I could hear her and my mom crying over the phone and praising God. What I experienced that day was salvation. God had saved me and given me a *"Spiritual Awakening."* It didn't happen in a church. It didn't happen in a Bible study group. Neither did a preacher lay his hands on me. Nor did it happen in any religious environment, but it happened in a jail cell. God had visited me!

From that day on, I have never been the same. I've come to realize that it doesn't matter where you are in your life, God can save you and change you. I eventually learned after I started walking with God and reading the Bible, that God is no respecter of persons or place. Which means, it does not matter where you are or what condition of life you are in, He will come to whomever, however and whenever. Nothing can stop Him because He's God!

Chapter Eleven
"The Transformation Process"

Unfortunately, I thought I was going to go home immediately after I gave my life to the Lord, but that didn't happen. Instead, I went through a series of court dates and a lot of experiences being inside that prison, that would bring about a change in me. I can recall waking up around 3am in the morning those first nights, in the new cell I was taken to. This was the area where all the killers, robbers, kidnappers, rapists were. It was a one-man cell just a bed, toilet, and table, I was given a bible that I started to read and as I would read, it felt like scales were falling from my eyes! I did not know all that was in the Bible. I was so blind; I started seeing how messed up I was and how far away from God I was. It seemed like God was talking to me straight from the pages. All I could do was cry the whole time, just feeling sorrowful for all the things that I been doing and the life I had been living.

The stubbornness and pride that had me so bound up, I could feel it being broken inside of me. You see, when I was in the streets nobody could tell me nothing, I was just hardheaded, mean, full of hate and wouldn't listen to nobody. All I wanted to do is sell dope, rob people, be a gangster, and listen to hard core rap music all day long that promoted murder, drug use, drug dealing and robbing. I was trapped! That devil had my mind so messed up, I couldn't even think clear, but now God had a hold on me, and I could not shake it. He was using these moments to break me and humble me. Even though I had been to jail many times before, this time seemed to be the one that was going to change my life. Day in and day out; I had to go through what I recognized was the transformation process. It was very difficult because now, I was going against the grain, serving God; and it was not understood by everyone, or they even knew what was really going on inside of me. The opposition and persecution that I got from serving God was real. It seemed like every day, I was being tested to fold or give in to pressure, whether it was to fight or curse somebody out. Being that I was always the tough one, i t felt different holding my tongue; knowing how crazy I use to respond to situations.

Studying and reading the Word of God had started changing me from the inside, there was a deliverance going on in my heart. My mind was changing on how I see things. I knew now that I had an invisible enemy; that uses people. I had to recognize it for what it was or go off on somebody quick. There were great days of victory, but then days I fell also; having to prove a point to a couple of dudes who thought because I was changing, I was a coward. The crazy thing is I was far from being a coward, but that didn't stop Satan from using these fellas, so I fell into the trap of having to prove myself by fighting on a couple of occasions. Lord knows I was sorry, but what it showed me was that, even though I was trying to do the right thing, evil still would try me. So, after those moments happened, I had to regroup and learn to the let the Lord fight my battles, by walking away quietly and not feeling like I was doing the coward thing, but doing what God loves and that was disciplining myself. Reading those scriptures was really transforming my life and it felt good. I never thought I would change in that way, but it was happening, and it was happening daily! My court dates were not final yet and I recall going back to court in front of those judges numerous of times, only to have the District Attorney offer me a life sentence without parole. He had labeled me a menace to society and that I was not fit to be on the streets ever again. I must say, he was not lying because before I gave my life to Christ, I was a demon possessed Lil dude crying for help inside and nobody knew. Now, a change had taken place in me, and I was on my way to learning a new way of living, that I had never known before; to GOD be the GLORY! I must say this, the transformation process was painful, but also rewarding at the same time! You see, even though I had prior church experience when I was a kid, this new life with God was real and not churchy. I was living out the Bible in front of my enemies and spectators, in which some doubted if I would ever make it through those hard-pressed moments, but with GOD it was possible!

Chapter Twelve
"The Final Outcome"

Well now, it was time to meet my fate. I had been going back and forth to court so many times, I had lost count. It was time to see what the outcome was going to be. I was nervous because even though I was changing; I still believed, I was worthy of the life sentence the courts had offered me, but God was merciful! You see, I don't know about you, but I'm one who had come to accept my consequences for my bad choices. I knew one day all that I was doing; was going to catch up with me. My lawyer at the time had given me an inside tip, that it was going to be ok, but I still was prepared for the worst. When I got to court, I was shackled hand and foot like an animal. My mom was scared to see or hear what the outcome was going to be, so she stayed outside.

Seeing her face while I was getting out the prison van made me realize, I could not do this no more. We really don't know how much our parents go through, when we get in trouble with the law. Being locked up on a murder charge, possession of a firearm, possession of cocaine, and had violated my 5 years of probation, I thought for sure the judge was going to throw the book at me, but it didn't happen. A miracle happened! I was sentenced to eight years and being that I was in there for seventeen months already, credit for time served was granted to me. So now, I'm looking at about two more years, I had to stay in there because according to Louisiana Law, you had to do half of the sentence you carried. It was all a blessing in disguise! What I thought was the end of my life, turned out to be the most life changing experience for me. At that time, I was ready to do my time and continue developing my relationship with God, while I was there. Little did I know, God was about to pull out another miracle for me. There were church leaders coming to see me personally, who had heard and saw through visiting me, that I was a changed man. One Pastor invited me to be his youth Pastor, when I came home. This would be the next blessing and that was; me coming home sooner than I thought. I was still dealing with opposition that didn't stop. There was an incident that occurred early one morning, while I was serving food to the other inmates. This one inmate was being particular about his food, he didn't want any pork on his plate.

So, me not paying attention I mistakenly put bacon on his plate. Oh boy, this dude acted out so bad, talking crazy using profanity, just embarrassing me in front of everybody. My pride was rising in me. My first thought was to take the hot oatmeal I was serving and throw it on him and jump across that counter and swing on him, but I couldn't. God had already showed me that, He was to fight my battles, so I didn't say anything. I politely apologized and walked off the line to the bathroom, to pray and regroup. I knew if I would have responded the way the devil had put on my mind, I probably would not be writing this as a free man as we speak. It was a test that was so hard to bear, not knowing God had a blessing on the other side of that craziness. A few days later, I received mail and one of the letters stated, I had been recommended for early release for good behavior from the parole board. I was in total shock. I could not believe what I was seeing. What would have happened if I had responded to the ignorance I was tested with. God had a plan and I almost slipped, trying to prove I was still that gangster from the street. But I passed the test and not only I passed, but I was given that early release parole! God had sought fit to use this to change my behavior and gave me favor to come home early. MY GOD! I had done a total of 28 months incarcerated and what was looking like forever turned into transformation. I was released on 11/13/01, at twelve o'clock midnight. Nobody knew I was coming home, except for the church elders that were coming to see me. Not even my mom knew. I went to the church, I would be attending and got baptized around two o'clock that morning. I was so full of joy. God had helped me, changed me, and gave me another chance at life.

My life was beautiful, I started going to church every Sunday, I was speaking all over the place. I went back into the prison where I was and the street corners, I sold drugs. You name it, I was everywhere sharing the good news of Christ and how He saved me and changed my life! LOOKING BACK OVER ALL THIS; I MUST SAY, GOD USED A PRISON CELL TO GET MY ATTENTION AND KEEP MY ATTENTION. Now, don't get me wrong, it doesn't have to take all that I've been through to change a person, but it was well worth it! I had received my SALVATION FROM A PRISON CELL! WONT HE DO IT! HE DID IT WITH ME! He could do it for you also, no matter where you are in your life! It started with a SURRENDER! If that is what you want today, now is the chance. Just say, *"Lord I give my life to you I surrender all my life to you. I accept you as my LORD AND SAVIOR forgive me for all my sins!"* IF YOU SAID THIS PRAYER, THIS IS YOUR NEW DAY; THIS IS YOUR DAY OF NEW BEGINNINGS! Welcome to the family of GOD!

Made in the USA
Columbia, SC
07 August 2025

61066063R00026